DINOSAUR CHASE

by F. R. Storey
illustrated by Tuko Fujisaki

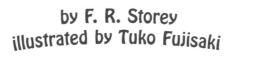

Scott Foresman

Editorial Offices: Glenview, Illinois • New York, New York
Sales Offices: Reading, Massachusetts • Duluth, Georgia
Glenview, Illinois • Carrollton, Texas • Menlo Park, California

Matt and Sarah were at the fair.
"Let's go on this ride," Sarah said.
It was the Dinosaur Chase.
"Let's not," Matt said.

"Someday I'll go. But I don't want to go today."

"Come on," Sarah said. "It will be fun."

DINOSAUR CHASE

The car went into a giant tunnel. It started to shake. It started to rattle. It started to hop around.

Then the car stopped.

"Matt, look!" Sarah said. Matt looked all around. He was amazed.

He saw tall trees and grass.
"These are dinosaur tracks,"
Sarah said.

"Where are we?" Matt said.

"Let's follow the dinosaur," Sarah said.

"Let's not," Matt said.

7

Matt looked at the trees. Sarah looked at the trees.

"Look! Duckbills!" Sarah said.

"They will eat us," Matt said.
"They only eat plants," Sarah said.
Then the ground began to shake.

THUMP. THUMP. THUMP.
"Let's go," Matt said.
The duckbills ran away.

Then they saw a giant head.
"A tyrannosaurus rex," Sarah said.
"They eat meat," Matt said.

It looked around.
"It is probably just following the duckbills," Sarah said.

The tyrannosaurus followed the duckbills. Matt ran to the red car.

"Let's go before he comes back," Matt said.

"I love dinosaurs," Sarah said.
"I like them too," said Matt.
"But only in books!"

The car went into the giant tunnel. It started to shake.

"Matt, let's go to Jupiter," Sarah said. "Let's sit in front again."

Matt looked at Sarah. "Hmmm . . . let's not!" he said.

Trip to Jupiter

"Let's not! Let's not!" And then
Matt woke up. "Maybe it is a good
day to stay in bed!" he said to his cat.